Mighty Mighty MONSTERS

NEW
MONSTER
in SCHOOL

STONE ARCH BOOKS

a capstone imprint

NEW MONSTER in SCHOOL

created by Sean O'Reilly
illustrated by Arcana Studio

Mighty Mighty Monsters are published by Stone Arch Books, A Capstone Imprint
151 Good Counsel Drive, P.O. Box 669 Mankato, Minnesota 56002 *www.capstonepub.com*

Library of Congress Cataloging-in-Publication Data
O'Reilly, Sean, 1974-
  New monster in school / written by Sean O'Reilly ; illustrated by Arcana Studio.
    p. cm. -- (Mighty mighty monsters)
  Summary: Being new in school is never easy for monsters except in Transylvania where all
the schoolchildren are monsters too.
  ISBN 978-1-4342-2151-3 (library binding)
  1. Graphic novels. [1. Graphic novels. 2. Monsters--Fiction. 3. Schools--Fiction.] I.
Arcana Studio. II. Title.
  PZ7.7.O74Ne 2010
  741.5'973--dc22   2010004129

Printed in the United States of America in Stevens Point, Wisconsin.
122010
006019R

In a strange corner of the world known as Transylmania . . .

Legendary monsters were born.

WELCOME TO TRANSYLMANIA

But long before their frightful fame, these classic creatures faced fears of their own.

To take on terrifying teachers and homework horrors, they formed the most fearsome friendship on Earth . . .

Mighty Mighty MONSTERS

Vlad

Talbot

Witchita

Milton

Poto

Frankie

Igor

Mary

For the Mighty Mighty Monsters, nothing was more frightening, more terrifying, more spine-tingling than . . .

. . . the first day of school.

Okay! Okay!

That alarm could drive a kid batty!

And next door . . .

OoOOWWWWWWWW

I hate bad hair days!

GRRRRR!

9

Is that what you've been whispering about?

No, we've been planning for today's soccer game.

What plan?

Our plan to beat you guys!

Huh?

Kitsune is a star athlete.

She won her school's Mon-Star Award.

It's really not that big of a deal.

Don't tell Vlad that.

He won our school's Mon-Star Award last year.

With you here, though, I'd say this year's award is up for grabs.

That's crazy!

Crazy like a fox?

Ha! I just meant nobody has ever taken the award from Vlad.

I'm not here to take it, Frankie.

I'll earn it, fair and square.

You were right, Frankie. This is bad.

19

21

22

23

A short time later . . .

There are four skills that make a great monster.

This competition will test you in all of them.

First, to scare people, monsters need to chase them.

This obstacle course will test your speed.

Who wants to go first?

Okay, Kitsune. Let's see what you can do.

25

Amazing!

I think you broke the course record.

Can I go next?

I'll break more than a record.

Okay, Frankie, but Kitsune's time will be tough to beat.

28

Listen up, kids!

The second part of being a great monster is the element of surprise.

Look out behind you!!

Ahhhhhh!!

Ahhhhhh!!

Ha-ha! See what I mean? Now *you* give it a shot.

But what kind of surprise?

That's for you to decide, my dear.

35

One hour later . . .

Let's see what you all cooked up!

Want to try a little blood pudding?

Dog biscuits?

Electric eel cake?

How about some bone muffins?

Puke pie?

Snot sauce?

Lizard legs?

Mmmm! Delicious.

So, who wins the Mon-Star Award?

There's one last skill every monster needs —

Yeah, tell us!

SPLAT!

Huh?

Monsters need to have fun too.

Frankie's right! Being a monster isn't about awards or competition.

It's about the reward of having a fearsome group of friends.

Yeah!

Sorry about before, Kitsune. You're a pretty cool cat —

Fox.

You know what I mean.

Friends?

Friends.

You're gonna get it.

Mighty Mighty Map of . . .
TRANSYLMANIA!

DEAD END STREET

MONSTER MANSION

BLACKBEARD'S SHIP

SPOOKY FOREST

MONSTER SCHOOL

FLAME OF HALLOWEEN

CASTLE OF DOOM

Mighty Mighty MONSTERS

...BEFORE THEY WERE STARS!

Kitsune

Nickname: Kit

Hometown: Tokyo, Japan

Favorite Color: Pink

Favorite Animal: Foxes (of course!)

Mighty Mighty Powers: superhuman quickness on her feet; cleverness; extraordinary leaping ability; super friendliness.

BIOGRAPHY

Kitsune didn't grow up in Transylmania, but she quickly became an important member of the Mighty Mighty Monsters. Her speed and cleverness are unmatched. With her love for all things pink, she also adds a dose of "Girl Power" to the ghoulish gang. Although this fantastic fox is already a legend in her home country of Japan, she has made an instant impact on her new home.

WHERE ARE THEY NOW?

In the country of Japan, *Kitsune* means fox. These clever animals have appeared in Japanese folklore for thousands of years.

In many folk tales, Kitsune creatures have magical powers and super intelligence. They can also have as many as nine tails. These tails show a Kitsune's age. A young fox might only have one, but an old fox could have many more.

Kitsune are famous for their cleverness. Oftentimes, they cannot be trusted and are considered greedy tricksters.

About Sean O'Reilly
and Arcana Studio

As a lifelong comics fan, Sean O'Reilly dreamed of becoming a comic book creator. In 2004, he realized that dream by creating Arcana Studio. In one short year, O'Reilly took his studio from a one-person operation in his basement to an award-winning comic book publisher with more than 150 graphic novels produced for Harper Collins, Simon & Schuster, Random House, Scholastic, and others.

Within a year, the company won many awards including the Shuster Award for Outstanding Publisher and the Moonbeam Award for top children's graphic novel. O'Reilly also won the Top 40 Under 40 award from the city of Vancouver and authored The Clockwork Girl for Top Graphic Novel at Book Expo America in 2009.

Currently, O'Reilly is one of the most prolific independent comic book writers in Canada. While showing no signs of slowing down in comics, he now writes screenplays and adapts his creations for the big screen.

GLOSSARY

batty (BAT-tee)—crazy or insane

biscuit (BISS-kit)—a small, round bread, often made with baking soda

competition (kom-puh-TISH-shuhn)—a contest of some kind

destroyed (di-STROID)—wreck or ruined

fearsome (FIHR-suhm)—frightening, such as a monster

focus (FOH-kuhss)—to make something clearer to see with your eyes

introduce (in-truh-DOOSS)—to tell the name of one person to another person

Kitsune (kit-SOO-nee)—the Japanese word for fox, an animal often found in that country's folklore

locust (LOH-kuhst)—a type of grasshopper that eats and destroys crops

obstacle course (OB-stuh-kuhl KORSS)—a training course, which usually has fences, walls, and ditches to climb over or get around

terror (TER-uhr)—a person or thing that causes very great fear

DISCUSSION QUESTIONS

1. Why do you think the boy monsters didn't like Kitsune at first? Do you think they liked her at the end of the story? Explain.

2. Who do you think deserves the Mon-Star Award? Choose one monster and explain why he or she is the scariest.

3. All of the Mighty Mighty Monsters are different. Which character do you like the best and why?

WRITING PROMPTS

1. Have you ever been in a competition? Did you win or lose? Write a story about the game or event.

2. Write a story about your own group of friends. What kind of adventures do you have? What do you do for fun?

3. Write your own Mighty Mighty Monsters adventure. What will the ghoulish gang do next? What villains will they face? You decide.

Mighty Mighty MONSTERS ADVENTURES

Monster Mansion

New Monster in School

Hide and Shriek

The King of Halloween Castle

Lost in Spooky Forest

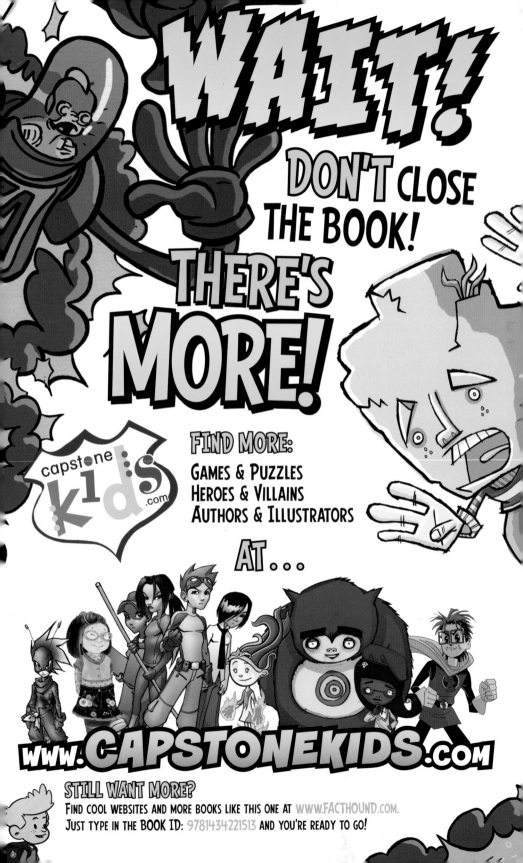